Secrets Hidden behind Closed Doors

Secrets Hidden behind Closed Doors

MARSHALL HANLON

SECRETS HIDDEN BEHIND CLOSED DOORS

iUniverse books may be ordered through booksellers or by contacting:

iUniverse
1663 Liberty Drive
Bloomington, IN 47403
www.iuniverse.com
1-800-Authors (1-800-288-4677)

Because of the dynamic nature of the Internet, any web addresses or links contained in this book may have changed since publication and may no longer be valid. The views expressed in this work are solely those of the author and do not necessarily reflect the views of the publisher, and the publisher hereby disclaims any responsibility for them.

Any people depicted in stock imagery provided by Thinkstock are models, and such images are being used for illustrative purposes only. Certain stock imagery © Thinkstock.

ISBN: 978-1-4917-8292-7 (sc)
ISBN: 978-1-4917-8293-4 (e)

Library of Congress Control Number: 2015919013

Print information available on the last page.

iUniverse rev. date: 11/17/2015

Chapter 1

The gray late-afternoon December sky is brushed with pastels ranging from the most lifeless of blues and the gentlest touches of soft purples. It's motionless, with no breeze to move along the blanket of clouds blocking the moon. A lopsided V of Canada geese crosses from west to east and vanishes behind a wall of leafless trees. The stillness of the horizon is suddenly lost in a wall of gentle snowflakes falling in very small clusters.

A single road coming off the main drag is covered with a thin veil of white, leading to a cozy one-story waterfront home. The front of the house is dark at every window, leaving no shadows against the chipless white paint. Flickers of orange and yellow lights dance on a small mound of snow at the back of the house. A shadowed silhouette stares out of one of the glass sliding doors—a woman's outline with long, thick hair flowing over her face, a warm winter's blanket resting on her shoulders and clutched close to her body, and a swaying nature stemming from her balancing on her left foot with the right foot placed nail down on floor. Her eyes aren't looking outside or at anything. Her steady nature is that of someone lost in the contemplation of a stream of seemingly endless memories.

"Come back to the couch. It's cold over there."

The woman turns slowly around, wearing a playfully devilish smile directed away from the window. "Is that what you call pillow talk, Patrick?" Her voice is husky yet sweet. She speaks with an obviously exaggerated but powerfully innocent voice.

"Not at all. Just saying you look cold." The couch is occupied by a man stretched out, hidden under faux fur. "Simply looking out for your well-being." The smile that occupies his words is genuine. The words are as real as the fur blanket.

"Mmmm." Her hum is heavy and follows a sultry sigh. "You just want me for as long as you can …" She steps slowly over to the side of his feet, clutching the blanket closer to her chest than before. Her voice, though, is sneaking away from the moment.

"I can't think of a man who wouldn't."

She drops the blanket, revealing the sun-kissed cinnamon tan covering her entire body. She arches her back and crawls under the fur blanket. She lies on her left side and turns to face the current occupant of the couch.

"You don't seem to be here right now," he says in a whisper hoarse with liquor.

"I just have things on my mind … questions."

"Questions, huh? What about?"

"A lot of things."

"Are ya gonna make me beg for you to tell me?"

"Fine. Questions about you and me."

"Well, why don't you ask …"

Her face wears hesitance as she turns back toward the snow.

"Go ahead. Ask me."

"So what happens after tonight? Do we return to the humdrum of going weeks without seeing each other and sharing small talk and meaningless conversations or …"

He runs his fingers over her hair and brushes her hazelbrown bangs behind her ears. "Whatever you have to say … that's what we'll be. This isn't the end of anything."

"How can I trust that?"

"Just have to chance it, I guess. Until you're sure of me"

"I trust you."

"I know you do, babe."

They run their lips together, and she crawls on top of him. Her fingers glide effortlessly through his sandy blond hair down to his rough-cut shoulders. He drags the blanket down her back till it's around her hips. The snow has picked up and covers the yard of dead grass and the roof.

But only most of the roof. One spare area of the roof is without snow, where a lone young man sits shivering. He's hunched over the skylight, snapping picture after picture with a very small, very professional camera. He readjusts from his stoic position, shaking the snowflakes away from his hazel-brown hair, and looks over the pictures on his digital camera.

"Yeah," the man on the roof says to himself, "that should be enough for him."

He dismounts the roof unenergetically, stiff from the freezing wind, and lands in a foot-high snowdrift. He walks for a few minutes, letting the blood flow back to his tired legs, before rushing away, driving his feet through the crunch of the compacted snow. Before he's a mile from the house, his footsteps are lost in windswept snowdrifts for no one to ever trace or discover.

Chapter 2

Each gust of wind that crosses the road throws waves of snow in scattered directions. Flurries pick up as the air grows harsh in the face of the man walking with his camera. He walks through the knee-deep snow, making high steps that hit his bundled arms. His head stays low against his shoulders to keep his eyebrows and lashes from collecting snowflakes. His camera is bundled under layers of coats and shirts; he clutches it every few steps to stay strong and ignore the shock of winter.

The sky is lightless, with the stars and moon disguised in cold, dark grays. The man walks without looking up to ignore the desolate feeling creeping in. He bullheadedly moves straight ahead without moving to either direction. Coming up to a turnoff that would send him to town, he momentarily looks back at his quickly vanishing footsteps. As each fills with another drift of snow, his mind is filled with the images of the woman clutching the blanket close to her chest. He lifts his head, and even though he's put a mile between the shore house and himself, he swears he can still see her—her thick hazel-brown hair draped in front of her face, her innocently mischievous smile, and her perfect jade-green eyes locked in eternity with his sad and broken brown eyes. The slow step she took to the window replays like a film clip in his head. He remembers how beautiful she looked …

A sudden rush of wind hurls fresh powder across the right side of his face. The shock of cold brings back the sullen grays and desolate sky. Those jade-green eyes have vanished from his mind's eye … he has lost his hesitancy. He returns to the stubborn push through the cold, leaving the thought with the drifts and clutching his camera as hard as his numb fingers can manage.

The snow subsides for a brief spell, and the wind is the only remaining hazard. The roads are swept with snow, blurring where they end and begin. The snow is fresh, without the paw prints of winter creatures or tire tracks. The horizon is bleak and obscured by lightless small buildings. One such building stands on a corner facing the covered street, a mile from the turnoff at the shore house. A small man with a large gut and a receding hairline exits from the front door and turns to lock up for the night. He quickly pulls his left hand out of his coat sleeve and grabs his keys from his pocket. As his hands shake and the key misses the slot a dozen times, a voice cuts through the frigid air and grabs his attention.

"Bernie."

The man locking up, recognizing his name, turns to see a man walking over stiffly.

"Bernie."

"Who the hell are you?" Bernie barks at the figure walking toward him.

"I got the pictures, Bernie."

Bernie's lips curl back into a heavy and perverse smile. His eyes widen into a long, far stare at the man in front of him, taking him in from head to toe. "Morris, my boy. Won't you come inside?"

Chapter 3

"**O**h yeah, kid," Bernie grunts between widely separated and naturally glossy lips. His sweat bead–laden forehead is painted an electronic blue and hovers inches away from a flickering computer screen, decades past its relevance. "You know exactly how to capture these tarts when the shot comes."

Morris Frost stands quiet about arm's reach away from the sex-starved man frothing in front of him. He stares blankly at the screen as the pictures switch, his expression a reflection of his flaccid soul.

"Don't bullshit me, kid. Tell me straight: Do you think they're natural or not?"

Bernie's gurgling and panting laugh cuts any kind of response from Morris off. Not that he had one to begin with. The printer, just a bit away, clicks off copy after copy in a migraine-inducing monotony.

"You seem stiff, kid—and not in the good way. Here, let me get your payment and send you on your way. God knows what could make you want to steal away from this …"

Bernie rustles through rat-worn cardboard boxes strewn about on the discolored floor leading to a back room. Morris waits until Bernie is distracted by his backroom, and the dirty money he has to count, before approaching the screen closer, taking light footsteps on the weak wood. He flashes through the pictures until he comes across the woman in her definitive pose—the pose that flickered in his memory like a candle wick. The blanket … the smile … those eyes … he feels the draw to reach out and touch her image. His hands tremble as the tip of his pointer and middle finger crawl inch by inch through the thin, cold air.

"Weeelllllll … I see even Frost can get a little hot with the right motivation, huh?" Bernie flashes a greasy smile satisfied by its own existence. He steps triumphant and cocksure toward Morris, who has reverted back to inside his own head. Morris pulls his arm away and tucks it way behind his back.

"So … are they natural or store bought?" He laughs another smug laugh and slaps the bills on the young man's shoulder. "Just busting your balls, kid. I'll send you to your own plans and life soon enough, but before you leave, I do need you to speak up and tell me what you know about this little rendezvous. Name and history if you can …"

Morris Frost stirs away from the eyes in front of him. "Well ..." His voice is uncertain, almost wounded in delivery. Someone in a hospital bed would sound like Morris Frost. "Her name is Ciara Lancaster for one. Twenty-four years old. No family to speak of ... though she does want a family someday. She always talks about having a couple of kids, a small house outside of the city with Patrick ..."

"Jesus Christ, kid. When I meant history I was kinda hoping you weren't gonna give me her whole damn backstory. Just the essentials. Occupation, address, et cetera."

Morris felt a bolt of fear swing through his body ... like talking about Ciara was enough to show a little too much about himself. "Lives at 104 Moss Drive on the south side of the bay, and she works as a waitress at the Rough Waters dive bar up in Northern Bay. She's a favorite up there."

"Favorite indeed. And the Boothe brat is putting her between the sheets?"

"Yeah."

"Please tell me you have a picture of that." Bernie's quivering lips, dripping with strings of drool, speak these words with both rabid desperation and degenerate delight.

"Should be on the next page."

"*Yes* ... yes it is. Oh lord, what a piece she is. Must have decided to break off for a little vacation away from the wife, if you catch my drift. And what a vacation she is. That Boothe brat is gonna pay handsomely when he sees a few copies on his doorstep. Nothing sells quite like blackmail, kid. Then again, look who I'm talking to."

Morris's throat tightens, and he feels the strain of swallowing come over him. He looks over to the electronic blue screen and wonders if he's taken away that smile on Ciara's face. Then he thinks that he won't be able to see her again. He tries to remember her smile clearly.

"All right, kid. Five thousand dollars ... and worth every damn penny. Maybe you and I will do business again soon. And hey—if the Boothe brat gets real desperate, I'll throw a little extra your way. Just don't say no one is looking out for ya. I'm gonna hand deliver those pictures on to his doorstep, kid ... tomorrow morning."

Bernie disappears into his own plans of grandiose piles of money and starts a long conversation with himself. Morris starts toward the door, uneasy, still feeling the strain of his throat. The hesitation of each slow footstep is holding onto Morris and dragging him toward what he wants. He turns without lifting his head and pulls a single copy from the printer to stuff into his winter coat. He does so carefully enough to not crumple the face. He looks back over his shoulder and hopes he isn't punished with another of Bernie's smug grins. But Bernie has retired into a room unfamiliar to Morris, letting his mind wander through each new perverted idea that can make its way into his head.

The drifts are past knee height, and the snowfall has continued. A fresh gust of strong wind slaps the buildings and hurls snow across the windowsills and rusty gutters. All but Morris's eyes are hidden from the elements as he pushes through the windswept, asymmetric snowdrifts. He places the picture between his camera and his chest to keep it from falling. Ciara's eyes play tricks with him, jumping into his imagination and running across the angelic white snow for the briefest of moments.

The barren windows of the former buildings morph into the neon-lit set of late-night destinations for the meek lives of desperate men and women. Morris passes a late-night diner, two bars called DeStefano's Place and The Mill, and The Cinnamon Shack strip joint fresh with early-morning catcalls before he sets his eyes on his own destination. The doors of Outskirt's Liquor open as Morris steps within reach of the sensor. He immediately directs his attention to the left counter and the smiling face behind it.

"Well, if it isn't Frost—right on schedule too." The man behind the counter smiles a familiar smile to Morris, who answers it with one of his own.

"Hello, Manny. You got my usual in the back?"

"Ah, I see we aren't quick to conversation tonight. So different for the ever-talkative Morris Frost." The sarcastic tone slips out instinctually from the midfifties owner.

"So is that a no or—"

"Don't you get impatient with me … but yeah, it is. I'll be right back."

"Thanks, Manny. Don't take long."

"Oh, so the man does speak. Well, this here oughta shut you up. Irish Honey—your favorite whiskey."

"Happy to hear. It's been a long night."

"Burning the midnight oil is only okay if it means something to you personally."

"This was for my job. It wasn't a big deal." Morris hates what he does even when it pays well, but he doesn't want to worry Manny. Manny is one of the few people he looks forward to seeing.

"Takes a man to think that way."

"Thanks, Manny. Someday I'll buy more than this."

"You sharing that bottle with anyone else tonight?"

"Why?"

"You can call us even if you are."

"Well, I am actually. Her name is Ciara."

"That's what I like to hear. You drinking to remember for a change. Well then, have a long, barely memorable night."

"Okay, Manny. You too."

The doors slide shut as Morris tucks the whiskey into his coat pocket. He looks toward the bottle with a glimpse of remorse for having to lie to Manny, who always seems reasonably friendly without a reason to be friendly. Tonight he will be drinking, but he wants to drink to forget.

Chapter 4

Just on the other side of Outskirts Liquor, with a block of knee-deep snow separating it, a small section of unsubstantial low-rent apartments stands with the usual faces decorating it. Three men are sitting on the stoop, hiding from the snow and trading stories both real and made up. They don't have spare change jugs or the eyes of beggars; they would be offended by the title of homeless. If you asked them what they were, they would call themselves hobos: men without a stable income and no place they call home by choice, not misfortune.

The three hobos watch as a familiar face appears through the white veil of winter winds. The hobo closest to the door stops midstory and turns his attention to the oncoming guest.

"Seems like any other night to you, doesn't it, Frost?"

He turns to the hobo, looking less reserved than he was with Bernie. "What?"

"Home late with a bottle of booze nestled under your arm like it was your newborn baby boy … sound different from last night or the night before that?" His cold face works up a flaccid look of contempt numbness.

Morris carries a nervously confident smile as he replies, "Tonight is different actually."

"Oh really?" the first hobo replies with a near-menacing inquisitiveness. "How's that?"

"None of your business really. But I'm not going to be alone tonight," he says, lying to them and even a little to himself, hoping to get them off his back.

"Ah," the second hobo grunts in a voice shredded to a charmless growl by whatever is in his bottle. "That makes all the difference in the world on any given night." He doesn't speak with any inebriation in his voice. He has a firm hold on his clarity, but he doesn't look it.

"What's her name, Frost?" the first hobo questions with a smile on his face.

"Ciara … that's her name." No sooner have the words escaped his mouth than he wishes they had never entered his mind. "I'm tired, guys. I'm gonna turn in."

All three hobos raise their hands in farewell and return to whatever topic occupied their minds before Morris came into their space. For his own return to routine, Morris slips through the hallways unnoticed aside from the occasional polite smile handed out from passersby who don't even know his name. He arrives at his door and has the top of his bottle open before he brings out his keys. He swings the door open in rhythm to swinging his head and whiskey back. He closes the door without locking it, not feeling the need to protect anything inside but the camera around his neck. He passes the kitchen without grabbing so much as a glass for his whiskey and passes the couch without even a slim idea of checking the TV. The bedroom calls to him and the things that are covered by his winter wear.

The bottle of booze is a kitchen faucet to Morris before it rests stationary for a while on his bedside table. He clicks on the lamp with no shade, and the light dimly pushes back the shadows of midnight. The picture he swiped from Bernie falls out of his snow jacket and onto the bed. Morris can't shake the feeling Ciara is staring at him and doesn't know whether it feels pleasant or not. Her beauty is nerve-wracking, and he feels something crawling around his stomach at the thought of Bernie alone with all those pictures. The thoughts and worries dissipate at the reconnection of those perfect jade-green eyes.

"Ciara Lancaster," he whispers to himself just to hear the subtle beauty in how her name rolls off his tongue. "Ciara Lancaster."

Her soft-looking hips and not-too-long legs grab him again. As he grabs another long sip of whiskey, his head rushes with tired pain of the early morning. His eyes slip back behind his lids, and he lays the picture with care next to his lamp. He snaps off the light and remembers his few opportunities to see her, to hear her. He remembers the dreams of her one day getting out of this area and going to a dance academy she once heard of, how she drank wine and champagne only, how she …

His mind darts back to where he is, and he reaches for the bottle for one last swig to knock him out for the night. His head rushes with why he keeps thinking of the one face he only knows through the pictures he's taken and conversations he wasn't a part of. The full weight of the night hits him, and he stops letting his mind work, leaving the questions unanswered for the time being.

Chapter 5

The twelve o'clock sun is high in the middle of the oddly bright sky and throws harsh light on the snowdrifts. The normally harsh grays that plague Black Diamond Bay's Outskirts are dressed with the angelic, crystalline glow of the untouched powder. However, the harsh glow of the sun-bleached snow makes its way into Morris's hangover. Rustling under the silverfish-ravaged sheets, he desperately drags himself upright and tries to make sense of his spinning surroundings. The bottle of brown liquor mocks him on the bedside table as he connects last night to this morning. He shifts to the side of the bed and lets his feet drop to the floor, letting gravity pull his head to his knees. The rush of blood to his head makes the whole room spin again and reunites him with a familiar face. Ciara's vulnerable smile greets and soothes his headache before reintroducing him to the uncertain pit at the bottom of his stomach. He tosses the picture into a hangover's carelessness before struggling to get into his afternoon routine.

He slides into his warmer clothes and slips through his dizziness into the hallway. The hangover makes each step pound through his temples and pushes him to the wall. Sunlight pours in through the door window just before his unstable feet. He groans a sickly groan in anticipation of the pain of the sun, of the snow. Each step into the light sends stinging pulses to his eyes and forehead until he finds the door handle.

Opening the door to see the shivering hobos from the night before brings a hesitant shock to Morris. They haven't moved from their positions. The one closest to the door sends a sly glance to his inebriated guest.

"How'd the long night treat ya, Morris?" His voice is intentionally and ironically a loud and pompous declaration disguised as a question. He speaks each word quickly but takes his time on Morris's name.

Morris would normally stumble through a question from someone he isn't quite familiar with, but the hangover has leveled out his nerves. "I'm never going to drink again. Ever!" He means to sound earnest, but he shouts the last word, sounding sick and delirious.

The hobo watches as his conversation is swallowed by the snow and Morris goes down the road out of earshot. "I'm willing to bet he's got another bottle or two in him before the week is over. Just you wait."

The streets of the Outskirts are populated with regular sullen faces and desperation; the cold hasn't changed the people of Black Diamond Bay. The Cinnamon Shack is still in full rotation of selling its A-class talent, The Mill is still giving the regulars their medicine, and dealers rest happy and shivering, pushing what they can to who they see. Outskirts Liquor is in rhythm, with a steady flow of people leaving and coming in. Morris finds he has come at just the right time. He reaches under the mailbox at Outskirts and retrieves a small envelope stained yellow by worn paper and nicotine fingers. The envelope has no name, no address, but was in the only place people leave requests for Morris Frost.

The letter inside reads:

> My name is Martha Asimov. I've been under the suspicion that my husband, Victor, has been leaving at night to gamble at the Dead Man's Hand Casino. He's a reformed gambling addict, and I need you to see where he goes tonight. He always waits till I go to sleep or doesn't leave when I stay up to catch him. I don't know when he leaves, and I don't know how long he stays. He's late 40s, spindly, thin, wispy mustache, and about 6'1. Here's my address: 116 Compson Avenue. We go to bed at ten o'clock. What you find you can leave at my house before my husband gets back in the morning. Your standard fee will be sent to this same spot when the job is done.

Morris smiles rather smugly at the easily accomplished job. No investigation required; in-and-out job at its finest. However, that also comes as a slight displeasure to Morris. He pays the bills with these types of jobs but finds them to be rather boring. They grow stale quickly. He much more appreciates the long, drawn-out jobs where he has to follow the leads for days or even weeks on end. He likes hearing people's stories as a side benefit. It almost makes him enjoy what he does. And sometimes he forgets that he doesn't enjoy it.

With the envelope carefully pocketed, Morris walks away from the cold and lets his mind wander. The cold isn't harsh enough to drive him inside, and the hangover has subsided. He thinks of how much he'll get for this job. Five hundred dollars runs across his mind. He thinks maybe he'll buy a couple of nice T-bone steaks as a change since he didn't eat anything for dinner last night. He feels his stomach complain of a sickening night of booze and emptiness. He perks up to find he's wandered out of the Outskirts and is over halfway between home and the industrial section of town. His stomach takes on another pain, and he continues on in the same direction. His memory shakes loose a diner in the shadow of Rock Creek Bridge: the Black Diamond Bay Diner.

He continues on, trying to calm the voices in his stomach. He wishes he hadn't thought of those T-bones. He feels some of the hunger diminish when he takes a strong breath of the industrial section's air. The fire in his chest erupts from the cold, and the smell of the stack's fumes makes him feel like is hangover is back. The last time he ventured this way on purpose was to approach some business involving some of the well-to-do names that live in Wild Rose Beach. He hasn't been back since, and that was a season ago.

He feels salvation take its shape as he catches the parking lot and small roadside sign of BDBD. His hunger reemerges, but he doesn't mind quite as much since it's almost over. He runs the rest of the way and weaves in and out of cars that are parked in snowdrifts under the bridge.

The smell of breakfast food is the first thing that takes hold of Morris, followed by the quick, immediate, and overpowering smell of the lunch rush coming into full swing. He walks into the diner and finds a fresh-faced waitress with a smile that seems to be waiting just for him.

"Well, hello there, sir!" Her voice is bouncing and draws the usually reserved Morris in. "My name is Vanessa Burke. Call that if you need anything special. How can I help you today? Need something to warm you up?"

Morris feels safe talking with her. "No thank you … well, not necessarily. I'm just really hungry is all."

She flashes her winning smile and spins the pen from behind her ear and across her fingers. "Well then, what are you craving?"

"What do you recommend?"

"Well, we have a five-alarm burger that's one of our favorites. Bacon, pepperjack cheese, onions, tomato, and some habanero peppers cut up just under the bun. Comes with julienne fries and fresh pickle spears. Sound like something to you?"

"That sounds good. I'll have that."

"You chose very well. I'll have that for ya in a jiffy."

Morris looks around at the diner and even the people in it. Vanessa takes the time to look over her customer herself. Morris catches her gaze and assumes it's a passing glance. After looking over and people watching for a few seconds, he looks back to find she hasn't left her original line of sight.

"I'm sorry for staring, but … I can usually remember a face and keep the name with it. Your face doesn't strike me as familiar though. What's your name?"

"Sam. Sam Danielson." Morris never tells strangers his real name. Bernie and Manny are the only ones who know him by his real name and that's only because they knew him when he grew up in the Outskirts. Bernie would let his name slip now and then to add notoriety to the name and get clients but they never got to see Morris. His name is famous but he isn't. It keeps business safe. It keeps him unrecognizable.

"Sam, huh? Well, how come I haven't seen you here before?"

"Well"—Morris feels a lump crawl up in his throat and tries to keep the words from slipping off in stutters—"I live in the Outskirts and only come past the industrial section on occasion." He's happy he can tell some version of the truth.

"Oh, so how do you like the Outskirts?"

Morris feels confused by the question. He's never known a positive thing to say of the Outskirts. He has never known anyone who doesn't know the same thing. "Have you ever been there?"

"I've heard enough to think it isn't a place with anything to offer me. But I only hear from people going to visit, never from people who know the layout. What is the best part of living there?"

"Well ..." He really wants to say something, anything, to benefit her, but not a single positive thought comes to his head.

"That's about what I thought." She laughs and glances back to the kitchen. "Looks like your food is ready. I'll be right back with it."

Morris is surprised to realize that Vanessa has completely removed the hunger from his mind. When she comes back with his meal, she brings it all back and takes it away in one sweep.

The cheese has melted down the sides of the burger patty and the hickory-smoked bacon. The steam coming off the top is warm and even relaxing to Morris. He is hungry but he also isn't thinking. And not thinking is something he enjoys very much. And he doesn't get to do that very often. After the first bite of medium-rare grilled beef, he sits and savors each bite that follows. Vanessa keeps an eye on him through his meal, trying to read just who he is.

He finishes the meal and feels the relief of a full stomach. He pushes the plate away and watches Vanessa come and take it away. She loans one of her smiles to him, as she does to almost anyone.

"So how did you like your meal, Sam?"

"Well, you sure didn't lie to me. It was delicious."

"And that's why you should venture over to the industrial section more often. You can grab a meal here."

"I might have to take you up on that, Vanessa. But I have to be on my way for now."

"Well, you have a fine rest of your day, then. Hope you'll come by again soon."

"Thank you. You too."

Morris lets the cold run over him and walks out into the mild winter day. Vanessa watches him walk away with an inquisitive expression on her face.

"Hey, Vanessa—who was that guy?"

Vanessa turns toward the kitchen and sees its one of the usual short order cooks looking out the ticket window. "Oh. He didn't give me a name. Not a real one, anyway. He's from the Outskirts. Short brown hair, five o'clock shadow, mid to late twenties."

The cook knows no one reads people quite like Vanessa. "So what's his deal? Is he a good customer, or should we keep an eye out if he ever decides to come back?"

"He's ... hard to read. All I can gather is that he isn't happy."

"Sad sack, huh?"

"Not ... quite. He's not happy ... but he doesn't seem to know it. Not yet, at least." Vanessa returns to her routine, silently pondering one of the few people she's ever met who she couldn't get a good read on.

Chapter 6

The clouds roll over Black Diamond Bay and cast sullen gray shadows on the angelic white snow. The salt-worn buildings that were just moments ago veiled by the glow of winter are now gripped in scars of darkness. Most of the people are abandoning the streets as the temperature drops and the wind throws daggers in every direction.

Morris's face can feel every sting as the unpredictable razor wind cuts into his cheeks and brings tears to his eyes. Moving through the crossroads straight into the other side of Black Diamond Bay, the trees of the Outskirts and the sickly grass of the industrial section are now scarce. The skyline is taken over by the waterfront speckled with the houses of suburbia. All the houses are lost to the snow with their seemingly unending stretch of off-white gloss painted on their walls. All but one house, which seems like a ghost of antebellum life. As he moves into Wild Rose Beach, Morris is numb and happy to be so.

He follows the house numbers until he reaches the address: 116 Compson Avenue. It's a small house that fits snugly in with its hundred or so brothers and sisters that look just like it. He continues to walk but keeps his eyes on the house to make a mental map. There's no fence, two windows at the front entrance, four slider doors on the back of the house. It isn't waterfront, there's a tree with no leaves casting shadows on the front left side of the house, and both neighbors' houses have no cars in the driveways and "For Sale" signs. Morris can feel the burn of the cold air as a laugh bursts from his lips. He has the perfect setup for tailing him, and he can get it done in one night. Passing through the streets, he turns at the corner for one last look at the target house. He feels safe, especially in Wild Rose Beach. No one takes a chance on getting into someone's business, especially when they have secrets hidden from the sun.

Nothing more poses him a viable piece of information, so he leaves the suburbs and follows another part of his job just a couple of miles away. The cold air chaps his lips harshly; it's the only thing he can feel on his face. Its times like this he wishes he didn't have the profession he did. He would have bought a car years ago, but he couldn't work like an investigator without a badge when those types of people are hunted like rats in Black Diamond Bay. A car with legal tags registered to your name is all but a wooden box in the ground. The police have problems with the PIs that work with them, let alone the unregistered ones who don't solve crimes but just bring them into the light. The crooked cops hate Morris's kind the most. The honest cops, though few and far between, think of them as vultures picking off the scraps of miserable lives. The crooked cops see them as possible loose ends that can complicate their ties. Most of the dirty cops are mere pawns when looked at by the hands that pay them; it isn't much to let them go if they become compromised. To a dirty cop, a PI's presence means he might lose his piece of the racket … which is why most PIs find themselves either in Sable Road Cemetery or breathing deep below the surface of Eastern Bay.

Morris has made his way out of the suburbs and into the part of Black Diamond Bay he visits least of all: the casinos. Most of his business deals with the private interests of people trying to discover what others are holding back. The casinos, however, house only the people who are looking to show everything they have and watch it disappear.

Dead Man's Hand is one of the Boothe family's big-time moneymakers. Everyone who lives on Black Diamond Bay knows who the Boothes are. They became the first family of the area in many respects. They are seen as the Kennedy family on both sides: a quintessential American success story and a heavily shadowed myth whose origins lie in the shadows of illegality and underground dealings.

The head of the family, Henry Boothe, made his money through careful investment and risk on the stock market—or at least that's what the newspaper said. In actuality, though, he did make some considerable money though sound investment; he made a very strong and sizable profit when he started to invest in the police department. He was a sheriff at first and started to bust criminals and keep part of their territory for his own. By the time he left the police department and had made his money, he had owned his own territory to do with what he wished. In the meantime he owned the police and kept them at bay with donations and by promoting his own underlings. His investment in some of the local businesses gave him the backing to finance their crime syndicate status. His children, all boys, loved their status as the royal family and abused it daily. It was a suicide sentence to screw them over or cross them.

Morris isn't afraid of the Boothes though. He figures since he is so low on the scale and doesn't cut into their bottom line, he has no reason to fear them. As far as he's concerned, he is one of the few untouchables in Black Diamond Bay.

He walks in, scoping out the entirety of the entrance. It is far from Vegas or Atlantic City, but the grandiose atmosphere is all there when you enter. There are two tuxedo-clad greeters and coat men waiting for you when you come in. Everything is a bright scarlet or golden yellow—from the carpet to the hanging bulb lite signs to the sides of the automated machines. Morris thinks it's easy to see why some people become gambling addicts: it's hard to walk away from being treated and feeling this important. And Dead Man's Hand attracts more gamblers trying to make it big than anywhere else on Black Diamond Bay.

Morris takes the opportunity to get a feel for the area. He walks over to the tables and waits patiently for the sweating man who is resting his forehead against his hands.

"House wins. Nineteen to seventeen. Would you like to join in, sir?" The card dealer is dressed in the usual uniform of black vest and bow tie over a white dress shirt, but he is less uniformly cold than dealers usually are. He feels pride in taking someone else's money and watching his table clear out.

"Sure. Let me get two hundred dollars in chips." Morris decides to play out as a cheap new gambler and try to come across as fresh meat. And what better than a new gambler's bait, blackjack.

"Greens or blacks?" asks the dealer, trying to get a feel for Morris himself.

"What's the difference?" Morris, of course, knows enough about gambling to play dumb about it.

The dealer changes his grin to a smirk of self-satisfaction. "Do you want your chips to be twenty-five dollars apiece or one hundred dollars apiece?"

"Oh … twenty-five, then."

"Here you are, sir. Here are your eight green chips." The dealer follows with another smirk that he can't keep hidden. "We have a five-dollar minimum and a one-hundred-dollar maximum at the table. How much do you wager?"

"Fifty dollars."

"Sounds good." He deals his cards and then gives Morris his own. Morris has a ten and a four in front of him while the dealer has a six face up.

Morris plays without thinking, like most newbies do. "Hit me."

"Seventeen."

Morris keeps in his role. "Hit me."

"Twenty-three. Bust." The words roll so effortlessly off of the dealer's lips. "Are you up for another one?" He isn't as formal as most dealers.

"Sure. Fifty dollars." Two more cards come to Morris quickly: and eight and a king. The dealer has only a jack face up. "I'll stay."

The dealer smiles and lays down a five. "I'll stay. One jack and two fives. House wins."

"One more. One hundred dollars," Morris shouts out in response to losing with rabid quickness. He wants to seem a lost cause to everyone.

The dealer keeps his cool, though he is pleasantly comfortable with the outburst. "Okay, slick." He throws out each card with a twist of his wrist. The cards fall spinning in front of Morris—a king and a four. The dealer shows an ace.

Acting freaked, Morris looks at his cards. He sits rubbing his temples with his left hand and tapping his fingers in rhythm on his right. "Hit me." Morris looks at the dealer and down to the deck of cards in two darting glances. He watches as the smiling dealer lays the card down in between his pointer and middle finger. The card falls over top the four of hearts.

"Eight of diamonds. Bust." The dealer takes away the last of his chips in a double-armed sweep, bringing them to his chest in an unnecessary grand gesture.

"Damn it. You all … this place cheats … the whole game is fixed … I'm … I'm outta here."

"Have a good day, sir. Hope to see you again." The dealer is far from upset as he watches Morris walk away.

Morris keeps a sour expression on as he walks away from everything. He takes his jacket from the greeter with a quick swipe and leaves without properly covering up. The wind and cold take all the color from Morris's face; it can't, however, take away his smile. The dealer's mug stays fresh in his mind. He doesn't mind losing $200 when tonight he'll make it all back. Tonight the casino will pay out to Morris; that brings him a little chuckle under his breath.

The near street corner of Spade and Marlowe is starting to gather talent for some late-night rendezvous. Morris falls into the crowd of lusterless eyes and makes his way to a shabby motel.

Upon entering the motel, a sweaty-looking overweight man with his ear pressed to the wall jumps back to his post. "Welcome to the Satin Shades Motel. Are you here alone, or do you have someone waiting?"

"I just need a room for the night. It's just me."

"Okay, sir. Do you have a preferred room?"

"I've never stayed here before."

"Oh … and the reason of your stay, then?"

"Business."

"Okay. How will you be paying, then, and how long's your stay?"

"Cash and one night."

"Okay, and your name, sir?"

Morris stands firm and keeps his face tight. "Alexander Hudson."

"All right, Mr. Hudson, here's your room key, and it will be down the hall with the number fifteen on it."

"Thank you. Have a good rest of your night." This considerate remark is lost on the man at the front desk. He goes back to the wall trying to catch a sliver of the voices on the other side. Morris feels a sudden weight in his stomach, thinking about how someone might compare him to the clerk. He tries not to think of that.

The walk to the room is enough to distract Morris. The walls are paper thin, and each grunt and moan slips through to his ears. He passes one door and hears a loud snorting noise and a slithering groan of delight. Morris is happy to see the low numerical door pass him by. When the fifteen appears as Morris turns the corner, he feels a slight relinquishing of his mind. He enters the door and shuts it quickly to wait for the noise to settle. When the door shuts and he stands perfectly still, the room is quiet and tranquil.

The weight of the day drops into his feet when he turns out the lights and lumbers over to the bed. He drops his winter wear and drops down to his thick sweats and long-sleeved wool shirt. Both have a few moth holes and years from when they didn't belong to Morris. He drops down to the bed and lets his head hit the pillow. He grabs the clock on the bedside table and sets the alarm for nine o'clock. His hand sets the dial and drops meekly down to the bed. His eyes shut and flicker as the silence and darkness soothe the weary and sleep-deprived headache of the day.

Chapter 7

The clock reads 8:50, and the hotel room is the noir lair Morris needed. The walls are still and silent, and Morris remains motionless; however, now he is wide awake and well rested. He has been up for half an hour staring blankly at the dark ceiling that he can't see. He has been aware of the clock since he stirred himself awake and watched the minutes go by. Now the solitude and silence has worn out its welcome, and he feels the itch to leave. He presses the alarm off and redresses into his winter clothes in the dark. His camera is the last to go on, and with it he leaves the room and forgets immediately about it.

The clerk at the front desk doesn't notice Morris coming in through the hallway and doesn't greet him. Instead he carries on a long conversation of desperate whispers with the wall, addressing it as "her," "you," and "dirty girl."

"Checking out," Morris says, trying to keep himself from hearing the end of that conversation.

The clerk jumps back to his inferior professionalism in a sweaty grunt. "Yes. Um … that's … yes. Okay, um, you will be charged for the full twenty-four hours. You know that, right?"

"Yes, I am aware. How much?"

"Um, comes to … seventy-five dollars."

Morris fishes out the cash from his coat pocket, trying not to notice the clerk throwing nervous glances back to the wall. "Here you are."

"Thank you, sir. And have a nice …"

The clerk doesn't get to finish the sentence as Morris doesn't wait to hear his pleasantry; the clerk is already on his way back to the wall as it is. The night has let loose a lot of its usual characters. The corner of Spade and Marlowe has fresher faces luring out the wallets of lonely men. The casinos are starting to swing with higher-class patrons and their dates, most of them not even their wives or girlfriends. As Morris passes by a shadow-hidden alley, a flickering flame dances below a glass tube and three sets of trembling hands. Morris is far more accustomed to this crowd than he cares to think about and wants as much to do with them as he does with the people of Wild Rose Beach. He's always been one of the night hawks, but he doesn't exactly like his company.

The night streets are glowing with headlights blinding all the on foot travelers. Morris keeps his head ducked and tries to keep focused to keep from getting hit. He lets his mind drift along the road and take him somewhere else for the time being. The kind waitress and her slow smile jump from the back of his mind, and he feels comforted. He feels a little bit warmer with her gentle conversation replaying in his head. The burger follows shortly after and feels like the highlight of his day.

Then he remembers those green eyes. The picture he kept close to him on the walk from Bernie's. He remembers her cinnamon skin. Her mischievous grin is next. Then he's back to thinking about her eyes. Ciara Lancaster—he just repeats this name to himself a few times. Some of the conversations he remembers her being a part of start to replay—the innocent conversations he dreaded at the time but had to wait through to catch them doing something they shouldn't. She talked about coming from a small family living outside of Eastern Bay in a community with a name no one cares to remember; it was called Cotchrey Hill, Morris thinks. She was an only child and grew up with only a select group of key friends. She always watched people whenever Patrick would leave during a dinner date or secret rendezvous. Morris always felt better about what he did when she would people watch. It made them feel close. He felt like they might get along. She …

Morris stops the recollection reluctantly when the sign for Wild Rose Beach jumps into his view. He's into his business state of mind now and refocuses to remain professional. Under the cover of the dark winter night, he slips behind each street-parked car to avoid anyone making a connection that leads back to him. At 116 Compson Avenue two cars are parked in the driveway, so both of them are home. He pulls out an old but pristine camera that develops quickly and takes snapshots of both license plates on the brown and navy-blue sedans.

The leafless tree has weak and easily swaying branches that don't benefit climbing. Morris looks at his best place to watch and recognizes his loyal friend as the best option: the roof. The trunk of the tree buckles slightly when he locks his arms around it and takes his feet off the ground. Each arch of his back swings the tree with and against the wind. Each inch up that tree starts to knock the branches and rattle. He snaps one of the thin branches under his knee as he stabilizes himself between the top of the roof. His hands grip on the gutter, and he balances his feet away from the walls and windows. He rolls his legs onto the roof and spreads his weight across his entire body to situate himself. He moves his body so he is lying on his stomach with his face pointed toward the front door. He puts up his hood, watches the doorway and the blue flicker of a TV screen, and waits for any sign of change.

The mindless waiting has never bothered Morris before tonight. He usually likes letting his mind wander through ideas and plans, but not memories. Tonight, though, he can't replay anything but memories. He just thinks about green eyes. Green eyes and cinnamon skin. A fur blanket wrapped around cinnamon skin and green eyes. That perfect reflection looking past itself into the snow falling and letting the seconds pass by. Her slow glances toward the water …

The lights above the doorway flash, and Morris snaps away from his momentary bliss. Victor Asimov slips through a small sliver of a doorway and flips the lights out in a quick flash of memory. Morris watches Victor step to his car and unlock it before ducking under his hood. The headlights shine a brilliant light on the house and cover the roof; the lights catch some of

Morris, but his dark winter clothes blend with the shadows. The car creaks out of the driveway slowly without using the gas pedal. Upon reaching the road, Victor still refuses to use any gas and coasts along. Until he hits the turn that leads away from his home street, Morris remains motionless and doesn't even watch to see if he goes to the casino.

When he's free of the headlights, Morris drops gently to the driveway and crouches into the shadows between the parked cars along the road. He reaches the sign to the community and returns to his normal way of walking, only with a little more speed in his step. He doesn't think of the cold forcing his face into a numb, flaccid mask; he's trying to keep a fresh picture of Victor in his mind. His clothes were the typical lower middle-class dress clothing, complete with clip on bowtie. He had a cigarette hanging from his lip and a wispy, thin mustache with plenty of space above his lip and below his nose without hair. He keeps the image at the front of his memory just as the corner Spade and Marlowe come into view. He passes the merchandise parading in leather and stockings and heads straight for Dead Man's Hand. The parking lot is packed with high-roller vintage coupes and gambling addict sedans and SUVs. He walks along the cars, checking each license plate along each pass. He keeps the Polaroid in his hand and looks at it casually every couple cars or so to keep it fresh in his mind. When he matches the plates and discovers the blue sedan from Compson Avenue, he snaps another quick-developing shot, this time of the car and the casino sign behind it. Now most of his job is over.

He stays shadowed for the moment and waits just outside the view of the door men in the inside of the entrance. Each person who passes outside doesn't take enough time to notice Morris; they either are too above him to care or too distracted by the idea of hitting it big to notice anything else. A little after Morris's legs go numb from staying in the same position, he notices Victor at the front entrance talking with one of the doormen. He then leaves the casino and walks momentarily out to the parking lot. Morris waits with the quick-shot camera aimed at the entryway and keeps a peripheral glance aimed at Victor. When he sees Victor walking back toward the casino, he stays motionless and steady, waiting for the perfect shot. Victor walks through the parking lot, looks over his back right shoulder in the direction of Morris, opens his wallet with a few c notes hanging out, and proceeds inside, shaking the doorman's hand as he enters. Morris pulls the photo out of the camera and shakes it until it develops right. The picture is low quality and doesn't look professional, but all he needs to see is what he caught: the instant when Victor opened his wallet outside of Dead Man's Hand.

For Morris only one thing remains before the night is over. The casino and the corner of Spade and Marlowe are passing moments on his way back to Wild Rose Beach. The cold is starting to get to him now, and he has lost appreciation for the comfortable numbness from earlier. The dark gray sky with barely discernible swirls makes him feel even colder. Even as the community sign comes into view, he can't bring a warm thought to himself. He keeps his hands tucked in his pockets, trying to distract himself as the numbers rise higher—110, 112, 114, and finally 116. He retrieves the envelope Martha sent him, keeping his handwriting from where it shouldn't be, and leaves the three pictures of the car in the driveway, the car in the parking lot, and Victor himself walking into the casino. He places the envelope under the mailbox and leaves under the cover of the gray night sky; his night is over.

He realizes that the walk for him is going to be unavoidably irritating, but even that doesn't catch him as anything to break his spirit. With the job finished, all he can think about is what to do with the money. His standard fee for these types of jobs is $200 a photo and $100 extra if finished within a week. Even though it isn't much to some, that $700 is plenty to Morris. He has already paid rent this month and thinks about indulging in one way or another.

He remembers that restaurant, that diner, that he visited earlier today and thinks maybe he'll congratulate himself with a few dinners there every now and then until this money runs out. Then considers trying for something better, like a good steakhouse in Eastern Bay he saw while on a job a few months back. Nothing feels more like a celebration to him than a sixteen-ounce rib eye steak, a side of russet and garlic potatoes, and a slice of warm cherry pie for dessert. That was high class to Morris. Then it occurs to him that he can up his equipment a bit and get some better cameras. Seven hundred is enough for both of those ideas. Set adrift so deep in his head, Morris hardly notices the towers of the industrial complex obscuring his view. Then he realizes he's almost home, and that brings him more delight. He keeps up his normal pace and keeps making plans in his head with the decision coming to him when he gets warmer.

Suddenly he loses his balance tripping over something covered in a thin veil of snow. Morris falls face first into an adjoining snowdrift and feels a brief and instant shock of frost. He jumps back to his feet and looks at the culprit that ruined his bliss. The drift is high, but he tripped over something heavier than snow. He uses his hands to feel in the drift and feels something cold and stiff under the windswept snow. With his hands he dusts away the snow and looks … all he can see are lifeless, dry, beautiful green eyes. His throat closes off like it the night before when he saw those same green eyes with Bernie on the computer screen. On both occasions he noticed a tinge of blue in the picture. He sweeps away the rest of the thin snow to see cinnamon skin, which is now a pale sickly blue. A soft smile that once was there is now an open gape that spells out her numbness. Before him lies Ciara Lancaster—left for dead, frozen, and forgotten.

Chapter 8

The numbness in Morris doesn't come from the cold anymore. He feels hollow; he feels like he doesn't exist and never did. He has the feeling of just awakening from a dream into a world he never knew. And the green eyes that he just a few hours ago couldn't get off his mind have changed. He once held them as distractions of the highest appreciation. They were precious to him after so many months. Now they feel like nightmares he can't keep off his shoulder. They feel like the thing that keeps him up at night, the evil that haunts every dark, twisted journey in his mind. He runs from the eyes, trying to put as much space in between them as possible. He doesn't want them looking at him. He just wants to focus on the burning in his chest as he approaches the familiarity of the Outskirts. His home, Outskirts Liquor, the various passersby all fade to obscurity in Morris's current mind-set. His eyes set and don't divert from the dead and dark building with the one glowing window. The man inside will have his answers.

"Bernie!" Morris yells upon entering the lifeless structure. "Bernie! Ber ..." His voice chokes out from the dry winter air.

Bernie comes out of the back room with an obscure look on his face. "Frost? What the hell are doing here? Oh wait, you must be here for your cut bonus I said—"

"I saw Ciara Lancaster left frozen in a snowdrift."

"Who the hell is that?"

Morris feels his chest tighten significantly. "The girl you had me follow. The one who was with Patrick Boothe."

"Oh ... the broad? Wow. They acted faster than I thought ..."

"What are you talking about? Who?"

"Well, the Boothe family contacted me. They said the usual—that I was slime and street trash and all that shit. Then they said they wouldn't pay, so I told 'em the usual about how something like this wouldn't make 'em look good. So they say they'll take care of that. I thought that meant sending a crew to me, but I guess not."

"You're saying they killed Ciara? Patrick Boothe killed Ciara?"

"More like the happy family came together and decided that was the best course of action. Whether Patrick got his hands dirty, I just don't know."

"So how come I'm just learning about this now?"

"Well, I was gonna tell ya, kid, but I didn't wanna risk my own neck."

"No. About the chance of her getting the axe. They killed her just to save themselves and I'm just hearing about it now."

"It didn't seem important to tell ya. Besides, I figured you would be able to put that together yourself, kid."

"So what are we gonna do about it?"

"*We? We* ain't gonna say a damn word now. *We* are gonna pretend like this never happened."

"What?" Morris's voice had a fair degree of menace in it.

"Look, kid, we could turn this into the authorities, and maybe if we get a straight arrow cop, we could make a case for it. But that would be suicide in the face of the Boothes. They would find us and kill us. The pictures ain't worth a damn, kid. Not worth a life, anyway."

"You mean do nothing?"

"I mean look out for ourselves. Some dumb investigation backed and watched by crooked cops ain't gonna do much for either one of us. Half the police force is being bankrolled by the royal family of Black Diamond Bay, so—"

Morris launches toward Bernie and clutches his shoulders in his hands in a tight grip. Bernie twinges and jumps at the pain. "You act like it doesn't even bother you, Bernie. She's dead because of you. And it doesn't even register."

"Hey! Get the hell off of me, you self-righteous little bastard." Bernie struggles away from Morris's loosened grip and stands huffing and blustered. "You can put all the blame on me all you want, you smug punk, but her blood is on your hands too. I wouldn't have those pictures without you. She wouldn't be dead without you following her for months. Hell, where is all this humanity coming from? You're a professional home wrecker. You followed her and watched her at her most intimate moments and didn't think twice about it. You aren't any better than me. You might even be worse for not being aware of it."

Morris looks like he hasn't changed his intense anger and rage, but he can't fight one thing that is eating him alive. He tries to rationalize everything into some way of denying it. But … Bernie is right. He can't help but feel sick. The green eyes creep back into his mind, and he feels a knot tie up his stomach. He can't look up to see the self-gratified Bernie and his smile. He simply looks out at the snow and walks to the door without another word. The cold of the season doesn't stick to him at all; he doesn't have enough spare thoughts to know it.

He doesn't realize he's passing the sleeping hobos at the front of the complex. He walks up to his room and crashes though the door onto his bed. He looks up to see his bottle of whiskey isn't on the table anymore and must have fallen. He reaches down for the bottle, and his fingers catch a thin edge and grip. He pulls up the slim edge with the bottle and sees green eyes. He feels a tightening in his midsection, followed by a choking strain in his throat. He throws back a long swig of whiskey and relishes the burn. Ciara's voice plays through his head. And then her eyes. His chest and stomach tighten again and become unbearable. He realizes how guilty he really is. He looks toward the window and sees the cold, icy-blue shade that covers everything outside. He drops the whiskey down and lets the bottle shatter at his feet.

Tears run heavy down his cheek and fall into the spilled whiskey on the floor. A moment of replay flashes the last sixth months across his mind, and he almost swears he can hear her voice again. He can hear her saying she misses her family, talking about leaving the bay behind, sighing after a hearty meal—those simple things both don't mean anything to him and mean way too much.

Then the cold, sickly pale-blue crosses his eyes again. Morris thinks about how much he doesn't matter and how much he should have been targeted. How he wishes he had been so that she wouldn't have been. She was his day-to-day and somehow became precious to him. He didn't love her, but he wanted her to be happy. He wanted her to remain what she was and to know she was still out there. Now he realizes how little he matters; his eyes fix over toward the curtain cord on the window. His stomach writhes at the thought of this being his last night. He looks toward the curtain cord and then toward the ceiling fan. He feels the plan crop up in his mind and considers letting the night end.

"Bernie," he says in a choked yell, "you're right. I have no choice but to admit it. I can't change that. I mean nothing, and I meant nothing before that. I may have killed Ciara Lancaster … and I can't live with that. I know this. It's only a matter of time now and only a matter of how I'm going to go out."

He turns out the light and lies back with his eyes wide open, rushing with adrenaline. He runs through the faces he remembers. He thinks first about Bernie, then about Patrick Boothe, and finishes with Ciara when she would wear her mischievous smile.

"I'm sorry, Ciara," he says to himself with a tear in his voice. "I'm sorry."

Chapter 9

The sunrise is an amazing thing to watch on Black Diamond Bay, equaled only by its sunset. However, to Morris, the rising sun is a stranger that he rarely has cause to meet. On this sleepless night, though, he has watched the sun pour through his blinds and shed beams thinly across the floor and the sheets of his bed. A few brown bourbon stains glow with the piercing rays of light.

The picture of Ciara Lancaster on her last night hasn't moved since the night before; it's the same with Morris. He has spent the whole night putting together a few ideas and thoughts about the world. He thinks about the idea of having a purpose for once. He considers what he can do. He thinks about what he is going up against, and he thinks about the quiver he feels in every breath he takes. He isn't quite sure if he's scared or nervous, but he knows he has to put that to the side as best he can. He takes a long look at the picture and stops thinking. He doesn't need to be in his own head anymore. His feet swing over the bed, and he dresses back into his winter clothes. He clutches the picture and places it on the inside pocket of his jacket. He grabs both cameras and makes sure one is charged and one has film in it. He looks back at the room and leaves, wondering if this will be the last time he sets foot in his room again.

Morris keeps his mind blank up through the hallway and only snaps back to the moment when he reaches the cold outside. The hobos have gone, and the front entrance is completely empty. The streets are the same in this aspect; there are no cars, civilians, dealers, or anyone out right now. Morris remembers how early it is and realizes that almost everyone is asleep. After that realization he returns to his blank mind and starts to walk in the direction of the Cinnamon Shack. He passes it without even a momentary peripheral glance and continues toward the smell of the crisp, salty wind. It's not too cold this morning, and when the sun takes up the sky, it will be even better. It might even feel like a warm fall day if it keeps up. Morris walks through the barely there snow and kicks up small veils with each step. The smell of the crisp, salty air is stronger than it was before. The sun takes up a small sliver of the horizon when Morris finally gets to where he can see it—where he wanted to be: the docks.

Morris into the parking lot next to the ramp and finds the four people he wants to see. All four of them are dressed in rather large high-rimmed coats and have large hats covering their faces. Each of them is resting on a piling with his feet keeping him steady in front of him. The three farthest from Morris start to make gestures at him while the final one remains stoic. Morris doesn't approach like someone in need of anything; he makes the whole thing seem like he has known them his whole life.

"You four the Maxwell brothers?"

The one on the far left steps forward. "What's it to you, stranger?"

The middle left one steps next. "You in need of something, stranger?"

The middle right one steps next. "Need some directions, stranger?"

The fourth one remains silent and only occasionally throws a glance in Morris's direction.

"I hear you four can get your hands on things with no questions asked. That's why I'm here, and that's what I need."

"You need something special, stranger?"

"Gotta keep it away from others' eyes, stranger?"

"You got secrets to keep, stranger?"

"The name is Morris Frost." It feels amazingly unfamiliar telling someone his name.

"So is it pills you want, Frost?"

"How about some grade A grass, Frost?"

"Or are uppers more your taste, Frost?"

"No. None of that. I'm looking for an unregistered gun. No serial number, small enough to conceal, and I need it now."

The three brothers drop back a bit and assume a rather uncomfortable silence before returning.

"Well, Morris …"

"The thing is, Morris …"

"You gotta understand, Morris …"

The fourth one finally steps forward and throws his hands up to the other three. "We don't sell guns." He doesn't make eye contact and then resumes his position and silence.

Morris looks at the three talkative brothers and waits for them to return to their repetitive rhythm, but they return to their pilings, and only the far left one starts talking.

"We don't have anything to offer you, Frost. We have no business."

"So then where can I go to get what I'm after?"

"We ain't in the information business, Frost. Unless you can't count and don't realize it's four to one. Then we can make something out of it."

Morris doesn't get to react when the threat is offered. A loud voice thunders out from behind him. "That's enough, brothers."

Morris turns around to see a tall man with a dark complexion and a scar over his left eye coming in his direction. He has two people following on either side of him walking; they look like they are invincible standing next to the big man in the middle.

"Who are you, and what is it you're doing here talking to the Maxwell brothers?"

"The name is Morris Frost, and I needed something."

A mousy-looking tattoo-clad man steps in front of the taller man and attempts to assert some control or presence in the scenario. "Some nobody who thinks he can handle the Outskirts. Why don't you try to leave the badlands for the people who already control it?"

"Morton … shut up." The big man in the center with the scar sends an emotionless glare his direction, and he shuts up in fear. "You missed his name, didn't you? We're in the presence of an underground man. He isn't a stranger to the Outskirts."

"How do you know? Who is this guy?"

"One of the best professional stalkers in the business. I bet that's not what he calls it or anyone else would call it, but he is the guy who you go to when you want the edge on someone. He gathers information and can get blackmail on anyone. Hell, even the Boothes can't avoid getting caught by Frost. This guy has a reputation that takes precedence over yours, Morton."

"Seriously? This guy?"

"Keep quiet. So, Frost, you have something you need from the Maxwell Brothers?"

"No. I need a gun. And they don't have anything to lend me."

"Why do you need a gun?"

Morris looks up to see the face behind the voice relax a bit in an inquisitive nature. "Does it really matter?"

"Well, Frost, I never took it as your MO to worry about looking down the barrel of the gun. From what I heard you didn't need it. I figured you were better than that."

Morris doesn't show it, but he is surprised to hear how much his reputation is spread in the underground. "This isn't for business."

"Personal, then?"

Morris feels the green eyes burning a hole in his chest. "Yeah. Doesn't really matter though, right?"

"Who will be the one to take the bullet if all goes well?"

"More than one. I'm after the Boothes and a few others."

The tall man's eyes bug out, and his entire entourage looks to each other and him for some kind of explanation. "You want to take down the Boothes … and why's that?"

Morton steps forward with a fidgety, almost worried, frantic speech. "You think you can take down the Boothes? That's a death wish. You crazy or something?"

Morris doesn't look toward Morton when he gets really close to spitting in his face. He looks toward and addresses the tall man in front of him. "They killed someone who …" He doesn't quite know how to label Ciara. He hasn't had enough useless time to consider those trivial facts. "They killed someone who … was precious to me. Someone who I share a few select memories with. I found her just last night …" He realizes that it hasn't been twenty-four hours and she's probably still lying there. "And I want her to know that, wherever she is, she meant a lot to me." He feels a hard lump catch in his throat. He doesn't want to cry, but he feels a well of tears perched at the ends of his eyelids.

The tall man's mouth rests open, seemingly interested by Morris' story. "So something just short of revenge, eh?" He speaks with an understanding of the story like it was his own. "What's this girl's name, Frost?"

"I'd like to keep that to myself." Morris doesn't divert his attention from the tall man and keeps speaking like the Maxwell brothers and the entourage aren't there.

The tall man sends glances around at his surroundings and looks back to Morris in an understanding nod. "All of you need to get the hell out of here. Morris and I need to come to an agreement."

The entourage steps away quickly, and the Maxwell brothers shuffle away from their pilings. The tall man steps close and brings him close to the bulkhead. "You aren't wrong for what you're doing. Hell, I've done more for less and would do it again. But I have to ask you, do you know what kind of hell you're looking to enter into?"

Morris looks over to the tall man, who's staring out into the water. "It occurred to me. I'm a simple blackmail hunter trying to go face-to-face with the most powerful name on the bay."

"And it doesn't matter?" He already knows the answer and just wants to hear how Morris will say it.

"It's necessary."

The tall man nods a few times and stares down at the serious eyes staring deeply into the water. "Here." From under his coat the tall man presents a small Saturday night special to Morris.

"Why do you want to give me that?"

"Something tells me you're gonna need it more than I do. And I can't help but want to see how many of those rat family members you can take care of before the end."

"So this benefits you, I take?"

"More like it doesn't work against me."

"You're willing to do all of this and I don't even know your name."

"You know my name. Everyone knows my name. You just don't know it's my name."

Morris stops and checks each side of his mind to reach some kind of conclusion.

"My name is Blind Bishop Lynch."

Morris goes wide eyed for a second and feels a stinging fear creep over him. "Blind … Bishop …" The scar over Lynch's eye jumps out at him now. The towering awareness of his presence engulfs the moments. Blind Bishop Lynch—the most feared men on the bay. The only man the Boothes fear.

"Don't be scared. You and I have no quarrels, and hell, I even have a bit of respect for you. Not too many like you on the bay. Just realize that you know where you're going.

Morris feels the weight of the situation return to him and displace the momentary fear. He feels a twisting guilt that he even took his mind off of his mission to be afraid. "I appreciate it."

The entourage closes back in on their leader, and with that Morris turns back toward the outskirts. As he leaves Morton turns to Lynch.

"So what happened over there? You scare him off or something?"

"No. I'm not sure he can be scared right now."

"So what did you do?"

"I gave him one of my pistols. Just what he was asking for."

"You …" Morton isn't quite shocked but can't say he saw that coming. "You … really?"

"You think I made a mistake, Morton?" Lynch turns a threatening gaze toward Morton and waits for the stuttered response.

"No, no, no. I didn't say that. It just doesn't seem like you. Helping him out and stuff. That's all."

Lynch turns toward the bay and stares out into the meek tide. "I suppose I hate the Boothes that much," Lynch lies to his mousy side man, realizing how little Morton would know about that level of respect for a man on a suicide mission running off his own guilt.

Chapter 10

The blinking electronic blue computer screen is frozen on an image of a half-naked woman wearing her underwear and a shocked expression. In front of the screen rests Bernie, passed out with a bottle of rye next to him just within reach for when he wakes up. He occasionally starts talking in mumbles about women, their individual body parts, and what perverted scene they're playing a part in. He's wearing a plain black T-shirt that's just big enough to cover most of his midriff; he occasionally adjusts and lets the dust of hours of junk food puff off in little clouds. He's perfectly at ease in the surroundings he calls home.

A knock at his front door triggers him back to consciousness, and he wipes the drool away from his cheek onto his arm. He shuts off the monitor of the computer, but not before sending a single wink toward the shocked face looking back at him, just so in his mind she'll know he'll be back. His thick, greasy hands swipe the last of the food dust off, and he quickly checks under his arms to see if he smells offensive. The snow blocks the peephole he placed in the door, so he opens it just enough to make his voice audible.

"Who the hell is it?" he grunts in a sluggish, guttural voice.

"Morris Frost. I wanted to talk to you about the jobs." He raises his voice to overcome the wind.

"Why the hell should I let you in? You wanna try to convict me again like last night?"

"Come on, Bernie. Let me in. I just wanna say a few things. It won't take too long."

Bernie swipes the eye gunk out with his pointer finger and thumb and tries to think things over. "Why should I let you in?"

"I wanted to apologize. If you don't wanna hear it, I'll just—"

Bernie shoves the door open by instinct at the word *apologize*. "No. No wait, kid. Come on in. It's gotta be freezing out there."

"Thanks, Bernie." Morris steps in with a faint annoyed smirk directed toward Bernie. Bernie sees it but doesn't take that as special. Morris usually looks that way when he goes to talk to Bernie.

"So, uh, kid, you wanted to apologize or something I hear?" Bernie tries to play off that he heard anything outside the door that would satisfy him, a move that's pointless after the rabid way he opened the door.

Morris smiles a self-loathing smile as his lips curl to start talking. "Yeah … I did. I wanted to say that it was wrong of me to say you were at fault for the death of that woman yesterday."

Morris doesn't get to trying to establish a second sentence when Bernie starts playing games. "Oh, I thought that I was some scum the way you were saying things yesterday. I figured you didn't want anything to do with me. Finally starting to take some of the responsibility for yourself?"

Morris bites down on his lower lips and chuckles in a way to say he's giving up. "Don't start appointing yourself to sainthood now. You're still a perverted con man, if you don't remember." His voice raises in tone to a dull anger before dropping back to a slow monotone. "But as I was saying, it wasn't your fault she died. It was our fault."

"Well, really more yours than mine." Bernie sends a sly greasy smile in Morris's direction before starting to laugh. "I'm just messing with ya, kid. Here it's all water under the bridge. Now we're back in business. Hey, I got another assignment for ya, if you're ready."

Morris switches tones to a sly, shrewd almost whisper. "Actually I think we still might have something with the Boothe case. If you're ready to listen …"

The sound of Morris Frost playing idea man piques his interest. He turns to see he's staring down a man with confidence instead of a silent kid. "All right, kid. I mean Morris. I'm listening."

"We can't blackmail them with the photos quite as easy. But we can get them for the death of the girl. We have something linking them together … my pictures. We could threaten them with police action if they don't send the money our way."

Bernie scoffs at the idea and turns his back to Morris. "Kid, come on. The Boothes have half the police department in their wallet. We couldn't get a case outta that. Nice try though. I appreciate the ambition."

"But were not gonna send it to the police."

"You're not making any sense, kid. How the hell are we gonna give the cops the picture if we don't give 'em the damn picture?"

"We send it to the *Black Diamond Bay Chronicle* and have it published alongside a picture of her dead body.

Bernie perks up at the idea and turns back to face Morris. "You mean to expose them?"

"We threaten them with the offer to expose them and trade money for the negatives. If they refuse, we send them immediately to the paper."

"And what if they try to strong-arm us?"

"We tell 'em that I have the negatives stashed away from them and that they won't be cleared until they get them from me. By that time we'll have a way out I bet."

"How will they know we're serious?"

"We use my name. It's got just enough notoriety on it to scare them. They know I can get those pictures."

"I don't know, kid. I'm still a little shaky."

Morris stops and lets his thoughts collect for a second. He never guessed a man who had his name attached to blackmail and pornography would ever turn shy. Then the thought occurs. "What about this?" He pulls out his newly acquired weapon.

"That ain't much for protection, kid, though it's a start."

Morris flashes a winning smile to his employer. "It was given to me by Blind Bishop Lynch."

Bernie stops worrying and turns to the frightening enigma of what Morris just said. "Blind Bishop Lynch ... that's his gun?"

"He gave it to me in support of my goal."

"Are you telling me we have the most dangerous man on Black Diamond Bay on our side?"

"Interested yet?"

"Damn, kid, you're a freaking genius!" Bernie starts heavily salivating at the very idea. "Here I'll make the call right now so we have time to ship the pictures to the paper." Bernie frantically dials the phone and drums his fingers on the desk, waiting for someone to pick up. He answers the phone and starts smiling ear to ear.

"Yes, hello? This is the guy who called the other day about some pictures you and yours would be interested in ... yeah ... yeah not from a phone you can trace ... ha, ha, I bet you could, you smug son of a bitch, but listen—here's the new offer: send us the money or we send the pictures of Ms. Lan ... Lan ..." He looks over to Morris for the rest of her name. "Ms. Lancaster to the paper followed by a picture of her in the fresh powder ... you might have a lot of cops on the take, but you don't have all of 'em, and that's just enough to worry you, isn't it ... ha, ha proof: does the name Morris Frost jump out at ya? Yes, I do have him ... if you aren't willing to play ball then you better hope the young Boothe has good lawyer or doesn't get sloppy ... All right, then try it and see what happens. We have the negatives and they will find their way to them even if you try something ... All right, we will meet to discuss it ... before two o clock tomorrow ... Sounds good ... Yeah ... Good-bye."

Bernie drops back and smiles triumphantly from ear to ear. "Goddamn it, kid, you are a genius. They took every punch until they heard your name. You did it. You're a—"

The Saturday night special fires a loud shot into the back of Bernie's head. Skull fragments coat his computer and desk in a thin to chunky red film. Two more follow into his chest. His arms drop down to his sides and stay there.

"Good-bye, Bernie. No hard feelings."

Morris tucks the gun back into his coat and leaves into the cold. His mind is rushing with what happens next. He ventures out into the cold embrace as the wind slaps him in the face. He doesn't bother shutting the door.

Chapter 11

The moment catches up with Morris in what seems like a crawling eternity. He drops down into the snow and rests his shoulders against the brick wall. He's never killed a man before. He never thought it was possible. Bernie's head dropping and its sickening thud is playing through Morris's mind like an unending film loop. It's a feeling in the same family as when he found Ciara but significantly weaker. His head is throbbing, and he feels nausea overtake him. It's not as strong as with Ciara but still enough to shake him. It's cold outside, but beads of sweat trickle down his temple and catch on his cheek. It's a cold sweat; he can feel it even on his numb, frigid face.

The flashing of red and blue shines off the snowdrifts and redirects the attention of Morris. He wonders why they're here on a nondescript day like today. He brings himself upright again and walks to the side of the building, peering toward the lights taking over the morning. His apartment complex is a parking lot for squad cars. There are men looking over the grounds and even harassing the hobos who have returned to the stoop.

Morris shudders at the realization of the Boothes' influence. They had his lease under their thumb long before this. They knew where he lived and could have had him at any moment. As good as Morris is, even he has never been safe from the Boothes' reach. He just wasn't important enough for them to take notice of.

Snapping out of the chill running down his spine, Morris considers his options. All of them leave him with few options toward attaining his total goal. He sneaks out of sight using the mounds of snow as coverage and makes his way to the Outskirts Liquor parking lot. He turns his attention back to the sea of flashing red and blue lights before regrouping.

"Hey. Hold on there."

Morris hears a voice boom out in his direction coming from behind him. He turns to find a man in his early forties wearing a worn gray trench coat approaching with his face braced down away from the cold wind.

"Me?" Morris answers with a chattering confusion.

"I want to ask you a few questions. Just take a moment." The man had signs of sleeplessness to him with his bloodshot eyes and two days of unshaven scruff. His voice was rougher than it had been when he was trying to get Morris's attention. It was gravelly but not from alcohol like most rough voices were.

"I'm kinda in a hurry. Excuse me." Morris redirects himself toward the liquor store to collect his thoughts as planned.

"Well then, why don't you explain that piece your keeping in that coat of yours?" the man asks with a sincere frankness. He treats the fact like it was never something to discover but was instead out for anyone to see.

"My …" Morris starts his sentence with an inquisitive inflection that is quickly noticed and silenced by the man.

"Don't try to drag this out with innocence you and I both know is a plastic fantasy. My name is Detective Charles Clover. So now you know that I'm not the person to lie to." His hands don't leave his pockets, but Morris is afraid of how steady he is. His unpredictability frightens Morris considering he knows the detective is aware of his weapon.

"How did you …" Morris is shaken to have someone get such a jump on him so quickly. He's a man whose best tool is anonymity and yet the detective has already figured out too much. At least too much for Morris's comfort.

"I saw you crouching behind the snowbanks. You were walking with only one arm out and the other one pulled tight to your thigh in your pocket. It's a rookie's gun posture. That or someone guilty and nervous."

Morris feels a lump appear in his throat and feels his fingers wrap around the Saturday night special. "Well …"

Detective Clover puts his hands up to signal for Morris to stop talking. "If you plan on trying to kill me, now's not the time to do it."

Morris is stopped dead when he hears the words escape Detective Clover's lips. His hand remains on the gun but is now shaking. His already shattered nerves are being played expertly, and he can't do a thing to stop it.

Detective Clover walks slowly over and pulls his hands out to get some hot air on his fingers. He rubs them together to gather friction and then in one solid motion lands a hard punch right into Morris's jaw. Morris staggers back and feels his arm pulled out of his pocket. He loses grip on the gun and watches it drop to the cold snow.

"Ah," Detective Clover huffs, "so you were carrying a Saturday night, huh?" He reaches down and picks up the gun, keeping an eye on Morris. Morris for his part makes a movement toward the gun but realizes he is outclassed and instead remains static in the snow. "Three empty chambers too. Was someone the recipient of those three bullets?" Clover's tone is menacing and without deceitfulness. He stares into Morris's eyes and sees a nervous panic staring back.

Ciara's eyes flash back into Morris's memory for a split second. He feels comforted that he could see them again. Then his stomach churns as he feels racked with guilt. He has so much more to do, and now he just has those empty promises laughing at him—the empty promises made to Ciara's memory. He feels like a failure.

"Yes. I shot the man who operates that print shop over there in the brick building. Once in the head and twice in the back. He's dead." Just admitting to it makes the feeling all the more real to Morris. Ciara's eyes run through his mind. They look sad to him. Like they come from a face that's been let down.

Detective Clover remains silent for a moment and turns toward the print shop. "So you shot Bernie, then?"

"Yeah. I did."

Detective Clover eyes the gun and then goes to Morris. "What's your name, kid?"

"Morris Frost."

He looks over Morris a second time and sighs an irritated sigh. "Get up. And get the hell out of here."

Morris's shock is written all over his face as he rises. "What?"

"Bernie Gorsky was nothing but a perv without a proper racket to get notorious. And damn if he didn't irritate the hell out of me. I almost caught him with some home pornography business he started with illegally taken photos, but he caught on and shut everything down before I could catch enough evidence. I won't shed a tear for him, but I ain't the kind to cut breaks. Now go get the hell out of here. Now!"

Morris gathers his thoughts and feels the courage and carelessness return to him. "Thank you. But I need my gun back"

Clover snorts a deep, disgruntled stream of air at Morris's request. His voice remains bitter through each word. "Morris, I know you are well known around here. Hell, the only reason I can tell you're not bullshitting me right now is that you're just the type of guy that Bernie would allow close enough to actually kill him. But your connection to him should be enough for me to drag you in with a pair of silver bracelets. Hell, nothing you do makes me think you deserve any kind of sympathy from me. So don't try to think that this is out of fear or respect, 'cause neither could be further from the truth. I'm letting you go 'cause you just delivered me some good news."

Morris sees the honesty in Clover's eyes; he isn't afraid of it as much as just amazed to see it.

A police officer walks up from Morris's apartment. "Hey, Clover!"

"What? Who wants me?"

"What are you doing here?"

"Ah, Officer Jameson. No one better to waste my time. I was getting some fresh air, and I saw an army of squad cars storming the barracks of this desperate ghetto. Figured I'd see why."

"Routine call. Nothing special."

"A call sanctioned by Police Chief Jameson leading to damn near a dozen officers running through some nowhere building and under shady circumstances … for your lot that actually is nothing special, isn't it?"

The officer is flustered and obviously aggravated. "Get off your high horse, Clover, and come down to earth with the rest of us. Now who is this on the ground?"

Morris throws a fast glance up at Clover. If he gives this officer his name, things will get complicated quickly. "He's a nobody. Why?"

"Hey, you—you live in that building over there?"

Morris feels no danger in answering. "Yeah."

"You know a Morris Frost?"

"I've heard of him."

Clover's eyes look over the officer in a judgmental squint. "Why the hell are you chasing Morris Frost?"

"Orders, Clover. If you bothered to listen to them for a change than maybe you would understand why I follow them."

"Orders, eh?"

"Yeah. Matter of fact, I'll get back to catching that punk and quit wasting time on you and this sorry bum."

The officer walks away, and Clover redirects his judgment toward Morris. "Why are these officers after you?"

Morris is thrown for a moment. "Well … I did just kill …"

"No," Clover menacingly growls. "What did you do recently? What did you do that would gather Boothe attention?"

Morris doesn't want to let slip his plan to anyone but doesn't feel a choice in the matter. "I have business with them."

"Business?"

"The kind of business where I need that revolver."

Clover doesn't say another word to Morris. He drops the gun into Morris's hand and walks away. His head doesn't turn.

Morris has a sudden realization. "Detective …"

Clover stops in his tracks but stays facing the same direction.

"Come by here tomorrow. Whether I'm here or not."

Clover doesn't respond and just keeps walking.

Morris pulls the revolver back into his coat and turns toward the apartment complex. The wind blows through, removing his footprints like they were never there.

Chapter 12

The squad cars empty out in a caravan of disappointment at the apartment complex. With the sight of the lights disappearing, the three hobos on the front stoop return to the conversation they were having before the interruption.

"Them boys are after Frost it seems," says the hobo farthest from the door in a relaxed, slow ramble. "Any of you care to venture a guess why …"

The hobo closest to the door sits up at this conversation starter. His voice is more direct and monotone. "Maybe he got busted … seems like everyone gets busted for something or another eventually."

The hobo in the middle stays relaxed and sips his cheap liquor through the conversation.

"What could he get busted for?" asks the first hobo. "He didn't do anything close to needing that many sirens."

"A man's life is his own little secret. Not like we knew him."

"Naw. That boy wasn't no angel or saint or whatever is your pleasure, but he couldn't get mixed into that kind of mayhem. He's too small time for that."

"Man had his demons. His liquor bill was proof enough."

"We all have our demons. Does that make him a guilty man?"

"Does that make him any different from the rest of us?"

Their philosophical conversation ends with the realization that the subject in question is strolling over to them.

The first hobo jumps into slight hysteria when he notices who it is. "Frost … you realize what just happened? Who is looking for you?"

Morris is all business and holds no emotion in his voice with his answer. "Yeah. Some officers are after me. I saw them leave though, and I won't be here long."

The second hobo doesn't change his voice to answer Morris. "You better not be. For your sake."

"Hey, you shut up now," the first hobo says. "Why are they after you, Frost? We need an argument settled."

"The police you saw are in the hands of the Boothes, and I pissed them off."

"Ah-ha. You hear that … you hear that? This man is innocent. You damn cynic."

The idea of innocence makes Morris chuckle to himself. "Listen," Morris says, keeping the same emotionless hush, "can one of you do me a favor?"

The second one puts his head down at the request. The first one doesn't hesitate in his response. "Whatcha need done?"

"I need you to tell a Detective Charles Clover to look under the mailbox in front of Outskirts Liquor tomorrow if he shows up."

"Absolutely. I can do that. You need anything else?"

Morris feels a tinge of sorrow take him over. "What's your name? I don't think I ever asked any of you your names."

The first hobo answers for all of them. "My name is Russell. That cynic over there is named Lawrence. And this drunk one is Jessie."

"Here," Morris says, handing them the last of his money, "consider this a thank you for what you're doing for me ... and for talking to me when I came home late at night."

"Oh please now," Russell says in a refusing gesture, "we don't need no compensation for anything."

"Then consider it a gift."

Lawrence steps up and takes the money from him. "I'm gonna save you some time and accept it on behalf of all of us. He will keep you all day."

"You sure are quick to take a man's money, even when just a minute ago you were ready to send him down the river with the rest of the degenerate bunch around here."

"Man never said he wasn't guilty of something. He only said guiltier men were after him."

Morris nods his head in agreement and appreciation at Lawrence for his act and words. "Thank you all," he says over his shoulder. "I mean that." With those words he parts from the group and makes his way to the mailbox, where he tapes something underneath and leaves in a hurry.

Chapter 13

The sun disappears at midday and signals for snowfall in the near future. The clouds cast dull gray shadows on everything. There is no wind—not even the weakest breeze.

Morris Frost is the only person on the road for miles in both directions. It's a quiet road—perfect for thoughts to wander. He takes a moment to ponder where he was just a few hours ago. Wishing to let the darkness consume him as a curtain cord leaves him breathless and alone in a joyless, whiskey-stained apartment. The darkness isn't so much farther away. It doesn't scare him. He doesn't flinch or feel the twist in his stomach. His nerves are steady.

In his steady mind frame, his thoughts clear away from the trembles and tremors that have plagued him. He feels clear and precise. And that is when the thought occurs: what if this is his last day alive? He doesn't stop walking but feels himself slow down a bit. The faces of all the people he has caught in his lens pass through like a clip show, most wearing devilish smiles or rage-fueled grins, while some are at the peak of bliss. He thinks about his first camera, his family growing up in the outskirts, his parents dying early; he survived for years after with only his camera. He built up a reputation as the best tracker and photographer on the bay, an enigmatic rumor who was never caught by police or criminals alike. Now here at a waterfront shore house, he is going to put all that in jeopardy.

Three cars are parked outside of the Boothe private lake house. One is an unmistakable Boothe car: a remodeled 1970 Chevy Monte Carlo with a matte black paint job. The paint job only the notorious can afford. The other two are standard late '90s sedans, one with a jacked-up grill and no left rear window and another with fairly good paint and no unsightly dings or scratches. Morris reloads and pulls the hammer back on his Saturday night special in preparation for who owns those cars inside. He circles the house and climbs the tank house tucked on the side. He gently creeps across the roof to the skylight he was cramped against just a few nights ago. He arches his neck just enough to catch the people when they come into view.

In the center of the living room, the white couch is decorated with familiar company: faux fur and a beautiful woman. Patrick Boothe steps into the frame and starts to whisper smooth, practiced lines in the beautiful woman's ears. She giggles and turns away at the fresh remark but plays coy in her own practiced method. Morris's blood rises at the sight of the smile that slithers from cheek to cheek on Patrick's face. He assumes the woman is the owner of the busted sedan in the lot. She slips the straps of her dress slowly down her shoulders, and Patrick snaps his fingers in the opposite direction. A second after the snap, four men wearing rough-looking, aged suits, one brown, one white, one black, and one gray, depart from the house and pile into the better looking of the two sedans. Morris ducks away and waits until he hears the motor rev and disappear. When the taillights fade out of sight, he scatters off the roof and runs up to the front door. The gun is tight inside his hand when he opens the door.

He enters the house and brandishes the Saturday night special by his side. Patrick Boothe and the beautiful woman cover themselves up at the sound of the door.

"Hey," Patrick roars, "who the hell are you?"

Morris pulls the gun up to his waist and keeps it rock steady. The woman lets out a gasp followed by a yelp and buries her face into Patrick's chest. She still faces the gun wearing a fearful mask.

Patrick tries to play calm as he starts to talk. "What is it you want?"

Morris sends a glance over to the terrified woman and waves her over to the door. "She can leave. You have to stay." The woman doesn't hesitate at Morris's offer. "Now it's just you and me."

"Look, buddy, what is it you want? Because I can get it."

"You can get it?" Morris asks with a vindictive certainty.

"Absolutely. Anything, just name it."

"You can get it," Morris repeats in the same tone as before.

"Yeah."

"You can get it …"

Patrick nods in a shock of fear.

"Ciara Lancaster." Morris's face is stone at the request.

Patrick's face harshens at the utterance of Ciara's name. "What the hell does she have to do with this?"

Morris fires a shot into the ceiling, calling for Patrick's immediate silence. "Shut up! She has everything to do with this. She's dead."

"You think I don't know that," Patrick says with a sharp delivery.

"I think you don't care about it. I think you saw her as replaceable. You let her die at the least. You are guilty."

"It's not like I was smiling with glee when I heard what the plans for her were …"

"But you didn't fight to save her. Did you?"

Patrick goes silent for a moment. "I … wanted to. But I couldn't get past the rat who took the pictures of us. Wherever the hell we were."

"You were here." He raises the butt of the gun and sends it in Patrick's direction. Patrick ducks out of the way and rolls over behind the couch.

"How the hell do you know this? Who are you?"

"Morris Frost." The delivery of his name is still a strange feeling to Morris.

Patrick pauses in disbelief at the claim. He looks him over like something will jump out and prove him wrong. "Morris Frost? Like *the* Morris Frost?" Morris nods, keeping his gun pointed at Patrick. "You're the guy who took the pictures of me and tried to blackmail me!"

"No," Morris says plainly, "that man is dead. I'm the photographer who caught you with her and now I'm going to get you back for what you did to Ciara."

"Why? What do you have to gain? She never knew you. She never even knew how notorious my family was. How the hell did she know you?"

Morris feels a sting catch in his chest. He feels worse knowing that she was just as innocent as she appeared. No affiliation with the Boothe name, as it's said across the bay. "She didn't. But I knew her. And somewhere along the way, I came to look forward to hearing her talk. Seeing her smile and laugh. I followed the two of you for six months, and she became my day-to-day. That was enough. I could have never seen her again and known she was still out there, and that would have been enough. And now she's dead."

A harsh knock at the door bangs through the house and sends Patrick into a fury. "In here! In here! He's trying to kill me!"

Morris pulls back the hammer and prepares to end Patrick for good, but then the door comes crashing open and the four goons pile into the house, brandishing their fists and various blunt weapons. The sobbing girl stands on the outside calling for Patrick to come to her and let the goons finish the job.

Morris fires a round in the direction of a goon and manages to catch the one in the brown suit's shoulder. He rushes behind the couch and plants to fire a second round when one of the goons rushes him and makes a move for the gun. Morris barely dodges and whips the barrel into the black suit's head. He pushes the black suit down with his hand and steadies the gun at Patrick. Out of the corner of his eye he manages to catch sight of the white suit with a lead pipe and the gray suit rushing toward him. He redirects the gun in their direction and fires. The gray suit catches the bullet on the left side of his forehead and halts the white suit for a second as he collapses against him.

Patrick makes a play for the outside and retreats with the beautiful woman. The black suit jumps around Morris's legs and wraps him up while the white suit tosses the gray suit off of him and lets him thump to the floor. The brown suit manages to get his balance back and stands up into Morris's line of sight. Morris throws another pistol whip into the black shirt and drops him in a slow, dragging thud. He pulls the gun back toward the two goons, who try to stay agile. The hammer comes back again and fires. The round goes straight through the white suit's left leg, high on the thigh. He yells out a horrifying scream and crashes to the floor, clutching at his leg.

The brown suit picks up the pipe with his good arm and hurls it at Morris while he again aims at the white suit. The pipe slams into Morris's hand, causing him to drop the gun. The goon makes a play for the gun, watching it go skyward. Ignoring the sudden fire going through his hand, Morris lunges toward the gun, and they both have a hand on it. Morris uses his good left hand to score a glancing blow on the brown suit's bleeding shoulder. He lands another two on his left eye and the bridge of his nose. The brown suit sends a hard right hook into Morris's jaw and knocks him off for a second. The brown suit picks up the gun, still dazed by the shot to his nose and the pain surging through his shoulder. Morris lands on his back and reaches for the pipe.

As the brown suit pulls back the hammer, the lead pipe connects hard with his temple, ending with a harsh metallic *ding*. The brown shirt falls to the floor with blood pooling on the back of his head. Morris pulls the gun away from him and uses the pipe on the black suit. The black suit shakes from the momentum of the hit and then remains perfectly still. Morris looks over to the white suit, who has regained his balance and is steps from the door. Morris fires another shot, though still disoriented from the shot, and manages only to catch his other leg. The white suit falls to the ground and returns to the screams of pain he had just recently silenced. Morris stumbles over to the white suit and looks down on him.

The white suit's voice has been reduced to painful gasps and shrieks from the two bullet wounds, but he still wears a sadistic smile on his face. "You think you have us … you think … you think you've won?"

Morris shakes his head and cracks his neck in an attempt to try to regain some steady vision. "I win no matter what. I made a promise."

"Well," the white suit says in a high-pitched yelp of pain, "you're gonna have to break that promise … 'cause you can't win here … you … can't win here."

Morris pulls back the hammer and fires a round in the white suit's head. He falls back, eyes wide open against the door. Morris quickly reloads his gun with the last of his ammo from Lynch and pulls the white suit away from the door. He props open the door and looks to see that none of the cars have left—not even Patrick's Monte Carlo. He walks out with his hammer pulled back and turns toward the road.

His heart sinks when he sees what's been waiting for him. The white suit's smile now seems more fitting. Four squad cars with about sixteen cops armed with pistols and shotguns are parked, with Patrick smiling in the center of them all. Morris stands still and looks over the end.

Jameson steps in front of the rest of them and starts to talk with a smug grin on his face. "Well, well, well … seems like I just caught the elusive Morris Frost. Now doesn't that sound good to me."

Patrick smiles at the imminent demise of Morris and stands proud behind the hired muscle. "This is what you get for messing with a Boothe."

"Now, Morris," Officer Jameson says, "I'm willing to simply arrest you and let you live out your years in jail if you just hand over your film of Patrick and surrender. I think that benefits everyone. Do we have a deal?"

Morris looks over each and every barrel pointed at him. "And if I don't, the answer is obviously—"

"We empty our clips."

Morris stands stoic for a second and flashes back to Ciara's beautiful green eyes. He relishes them, takes in a deep breath, and then exhales. Then he crouches down, fires a shot in between the officers, and catches Patrick with it. Patrick drops to his back with the pain of the shot. Blood bursts out of his chest and stains the shoulders of the officers next to him. Morris pulls back the hammer and lines up another shot.

"Fire!" screams Jameson. A sea of bullets leaves all at once in a sudden burst of aggression. After the first wave of shots is fired simultaneously, the rest of the shots are disparate but aimed at the same spot.

Shots pierce Morris's body and shatter the cameras dangling around his neck. He falls back as shots continue into his body and send droplets of blood to the once-pure, untouched snow. He crashes hard onto the packed white driveway. His lifeless eyes are skyward as the smoke from the guns drifts away in the wind.

Officer Jameson raises his hand to call for a ceasefire, and the guns silence in a snap. He walks over to Morris's carcass and checks the broken pieces of camera. He turns to look back at Patrick while taking slow, proud steps. He looks into the pain-stricken eyes of Patrick Boothe, and Patrick's eyes look back.

"Did he get ya, Patrick?"

Patrick's eyes scream as he looks up at Jameson. His voice cracks in the same gasps and shrieks the white suit used. "No shit he got me. Just below my chest. Oh my God, I'm gut shot."

"Maybe hearing Morris Frost is dead will help ya bounce back a bit."

"Serves him right. The dumb bastard."

"Why was he after you?"

"Honest to God, the man was crazy. He was trying to get revenge for one of my girlfriends." Jameson chuckles to himself. "Yeah, that comes with the territory."

"This isn't funny, goddamn it. What if this kills me?"

"Too low for that. Missed all the vitals. We'll get you to a hospital before the bleeding gets too bad."

"Does he have the negatives on him?"

"No. But we'll be back at his apartment later to find 'em. We should focus on getting you to the hospital. Men, get him into the car. Also, take Morris down to the shore and sink 'im. This whole waterway bleeds into Eastern Bay. We'll let the fisherman or the fish find him."

Two cops drag Morris's limp body to the shoreline and toss him in by his arms and his legs. The cold water rushes into his body through his many bullet wounds. He floats for a short period before sinking into the low, dark depths of the bottom. The current drags him away to float with the rest of the forgotten, waterlogged bodies in Eastern Bay.

Chapter 14

Aday removed from the lonesome, unknown death of Morris Frost, Detective Clover strolls into the Outskirts, embracing the barely cold day. He and Officer Eric Bennett are just outside of the projects walking toward the hobos.

"What do you mean a parking lot of cop cars?" Bennett roars in frustration. "Who all was here?"

"Jameson and some of the other criminals who you let have a badge and don't arrest on sight."

"You think everyone is a criminal."

"Just the cops. And most of the citizens. Not everyone. But almost."

"Easy on the cynicism. You might live longer."

"A long life on Black Diamond Bay is the ultimate punishment."

The two come up to the stoop and nod to greet the hobos. "Hello there."

Russell flashes an optimistic smile toward Bennett and Clover. "Howdy there, gentlemen. You all looking to ask us some questions again?"

Bennett steps forward. "No, no, no. Those men won't be bothering about that ever again."

"We're looking for Morris Frost. Is he in there?"

"What's your name?"

Lawrence states the question in a blank drone that catches the two off guard. "I'm Eric Bennett, and this is Charles Clover."

Lawrence nods his head at Clover's name and points toward the liquor store. "Morris told us to tell you that he left something for Clover under that mailbox over there."

"Thank you, boys." Bennett turns away with his partner and sends a sign of appreciation to the benevolent hobos. Refocusing, he turns his attention to Clover. "So, Clover ... your connection is the notorious Morris Frost?"

"Or at least someone who said he was."

"When did you meet him?"

"Yesterday. Met him when your men were raiding his home."

"What was he doing here?"

"Seemed to have a mission. Some kind of vendetta against the Boothe family. He ended up wasting Bernie Gorsky in the wake of it. So I let him go."

"That's all you needed to hear to let him go."

"I don't regret it yet."

Clover reaches under the mailbox and retrieves an envelope taped underneath. He pops open the seal and pulls the paper inside of it.

Detective Clover,

Enclosed are the negatives of an assignment Bernie had me on. I followed Patrick Boothe with a Ciara Lancaster, recently found dead, I'm sure, and caught the two of them in bed with each other. These are the pictures of them. Use them as you will.

Last will and testament,

Morris Frost

"Bennett … we've just been given one hell of a chess piece."

"What? What is it?"

"I'll tell ya on the way to the *Black Diamond Bay Chronicle*."

Printed in the United States
By Bookmasters